PLAYING
WITH FIRE

PLAYING WITH FIRE

Gail Anderson-Dargatz

RAVEN BOOKS
an imprint of
ORCA BOOK PUBLISHERS

Library and Archives Canada Cataloguing in Publication

Anderson-Dargatz, Gail, 1963–, author
Playing with fire / Gail Anderson-Dargatz.
(Rapid reads)

Issued in print and electronic formats.
ISBN 978-1-4598-0840-9 (pbk.).—ISBN 978-1-4598-0841-6 (pdf).—
ISBN 978-1-4598-0842-3 (epub)

I. Title. II. Series: Rapid reads
PS8551.N3574P53 2015   C813'.54   C2015-901564-2
C2015-901565-0

First published in the United States, 2015
Library of Congress Control Number: 2015934294

Summary: Small-town journalist Claire Abbott seeks
an arsonist in this work of crime fiction. (RL 2.8)

*Orca Book Publishers is dedicated to preserving the environment and has
printed this book on Forest Stewardship Council® certified paper.*

Orca Book Publishers gratefully acknowledges the support for
its publishing programs provided by the following agencies:
the Government of Canada through the Canada Book Fund and the
Canada Council for the Arts, and the Province of British Columbia
through the BC Arts Council and the Book Publishing Tax Credit.

Cover design by Jenn Playford
Cover photography by iStock Photo

ORCA BOOK PUBLISHERS
www.orcabook.com

Printed and bound in Canada.

18 17 16 15 • 4 3 2 1

For Mitch, as always

ONE

My boss, Carol, was already at her desk when I opened our office door. I paused before entering. Crap, I thought. I'd only had a few hours of sleep the night before, and I knew it showed. Carol would undoubtedly grill me for details about my evening with Trevor. The thing is, I had spent most of the night with Matt instead.

Carol sat back, looking amused with me. Her black blazer was a bit too small and pulled at the shoulders. She was chubby from years of sitting at her laptop.

"Claire, you have someone waiting for you," she told me.

I turned to see Trevor Bragg leaning against my desk. His muscled arms were crossed. I could see the ridges of his stomach muscles under his T-shirt. The guy was a hunk, *really* fit. But then, he had to be. He was a firefighter.

I suddenly wished I had taken more care getting dressed that morning. I had woken up late and grabbed the first clean outfit I could find, a blue T-shirt and jeans.

"Oh, Trevor," I said. "I'm so sorry I didn't get to the restaurant last night."

"Didn't you two have a date?" Carol asked.

"I never made it," I told her. "Something came up."

"Something always comes up," said Trevor. "Doesn't it, Claire?"

I felt my face heat up in embarrassment. He was right, of course. I had stood

Trevor up three dates in a row. Each time, I'd had to cover some news story.

I work as a reporter and photographer at the *Black Lake Times*, a weekly newspaper. Our town is so small that Carol and I are the only writers for the paper. I rarely get a full day off.

"Trevor, I meant to call—" I started, but he held up his hand to stop me.

"The chief told me how you saved the Miller girl last night," he said. "I ran into him when I picked up my morning coffee."

He meant Jim Wallis, our town fire chief and a family friend.

Trevor pushed himself up from my desk. "Jim said you had some kind of vision that led you to find Amber in the woods," he said.

He stepped so close to me I could smell him. Boy, did he smell good, and not just of shampoo. He smelled like a *man*. The night before, I was ready to tell him that we were over. Now all I wanted to do was wrap my arms around his neck and kiss him.

Trevor clearly wasn't in the mood. "I also heard you and Matt Holden were pretty cozy over at Big Al's burger joint last night," he said.

Matt was the search-and-rescue manager for our area. He had headed up the search for Amber Miller the night before. After I tracked down Amber, Matt saw me in a different light. He was interested in me now in a way he hadn't been before. I wasn't about to tell Trevor that.

"We were hungry after the search."

"You were at Big Al's until two o'clock in the morning."

"Matt and I were *talking,* that's all," I told Trevor. "He wanted to know about my vision, how it worked."

"Me too," said Carol. "You've got the town buzzing. Everyone at Tommy's Café was talking about you this morning."

Tommy's Café is the hangout for cops in our town. Fire Chief Wallis was there most mornings. Matt was often there too. If I wanted to find news, Tommy's Café was the place to go. I had avoided the café that morning, however. I knew *I* would be the topic of gossip.

"I hear you knew Doug Connor had kidnapped Amber before anyone else," Carol said. "Did you really see all that in a vision?"

"Yeah, but my vision didn't tell me Doug would throw my camera bag into a gulley." I was still mad about that. My wallet was in there.

Carol raised her eyebrows to me, asking me to explain.

"I don't know how visions work," I told her. "Last night was the first time I had one."

"Your mom has them all the time, though, right? Or she thinks she does."

I felt my face flush in embarrassment. Mom had claimed she had visions for years. I had thought she was a flake. The whole town thought she was a little nutty. Now I was sure they thought I was crazy too.

I'd always had hunches, but I kept them to myself. I often followed that gut feeling to the scene of an accident. That's how I ended up standing up Trevor so often. I would be on my way to a date with him and would *know* someone was in trouble. Like last night. I had felt driven to help Amber.

"I *am* sorry about last night," I told Trevor.

He brushed my hair off my shoulder. "Maybe you can make it up to me later."

"Knock, knock." I turned to see Matt Holden standing at the door to our office. He paused, taking in Trevor's hand still on my shoulder. Then he offered me a coffee.

"I kept you up most of the night," he said. "I figured the least I could do was bring you coffee." I got the impression he was talking as much to Trevor as to me. He was telling Trevor to back off, that I was his girl.

Trevor ran a thumb across his manly chin. "Claire missed her date with me last night because of you," he said. "Seems to me you owe *me* a little something."

Matt faced Trevor. "Well, maybe there was a reason she chose to spend the night with me instead of you," he said.

Both men were so tall I had to look up at them. I found myself between them as they stared each other down. I have to admit, their attention was thrilling. I'd never had two men fight over me before.

"Okay, boys," said Carol. "Take it outside. We've got work to do."

In the near distance, I heard the wail of the firehouse siren, calling the volunteer firefighters. "Shit," said Trevor. "Sounds like I've definitely got work to do."

Trevor gave my arm a squeeze before he pushed past Matt. Carol and I watched him swagger out the door.

Matt cleared his throat to get my attention. "I guess I'd better get going too," he said. He took my hand. "I would like to see you again," he told me.

"I'd like that too."

"Maybe dinner tomorrow night?"

"Dinner would be great."

"I'll call you later." He paused before leaving. "You aren't going to stand *me* up, are you?" he asked.

I laughed. "No, I won't stand you up."

"Good."

"Matt's cute," said Carol after he left.

"Rugged," I said. "Not cute." With his day-old beard, I could picture Matt in a log cabin. He was comfortable in the wild. As the search-and-rescue manager, he had to be. Our town was surrounded by mountain forest.

Carol eyed me. "Trevor is cute too."

I collapsed into my office chair, exhausted. "What are you getting at, Carol?"

"You will have to make a choice, you know."

I rubbed my forehead. "I just want to get to know them both a little better first."

"Matt is more mature," Carol said. She played with a curl of her perm. "But then, Trevor has really big feet." She was right. Trevor wore size thirteen boots.

"So?" I asked.

"You know what they say about men with big feet." She winked at me. "Men with big feet have really big—"

"Egos," I said, finishing her sentence. "I think Trevor likes being a firefighter, maybe a little too much."

"Of course he does," she said. "*You* like that he's a firefighter." Then she gave me a stern look. "Speaking of firefighters, don't you have somewhere to go?"

"Bed?" I said.

"The fire?" she asked.

"Of course. Sorry. I'm so tired I'm not thinking straight." I grabbed one of the office cameras. Then I jumped in my car and followed the smoke to the fire.

TWO

The shed behind the garden and pet store was on fire. The wooden building had housed hay bales and bags of feed. All that dry material fed the fire. Now the roof was aflame.

I took photos of the firemen as they sprayed water with the fire-truck hoses. I admit I took more pictures of Trevor than of the rest of the crew. I emailed several of the best shots to my editor, using my smartphone as a hotspot.

As the firemen put out the last of the flames, the crowd cheered. I clapped too.

Trevor tugged the rim of his helmet at me. I beamed back at him. In that moment I felt he had put on this show entirely for me.

As the men started to roll up the hoses, I walked over to the fire chief. "That's the fourth shed fire this month," I told him. "Have we got a firebug on our hands?"

Jim took off his fire helmet. "I hate to say it, but I do think we have an arsonist in town. He's likely some teen who gets a thrill from setting fires. Up to this point, he's only burned empty buildings where no one was likely to get hurt."

"But this shed is right in town," I said. "The other fires were out in the country."

"The arsonist is getting braver. This is the first building he's set on fire that was still in use. Looks like his obsession with fire is growing."

I glanced around at the crowd. "Isn't it often the case that firebugs like to watch the fire they set?"

"That's what I understand, but the arsonist could be anyone. With all these kids on their way to school, there's a dozen teens here now. The firebug could have been any one of them."

In the crowd there was a sickly-looking kid eating a breakfast sandwich. A chubby kid picking his nose. Over to the left, there was a tall lanky guy who must have been on the basketball team. He stood head and shoulders over everyone else.

Then there was a young stud in his late teens dressed in a hoodie and jeans. A girl with flaming-red hair leaned against him. The dye job had to be his girlfriend.

I felt that familiar twinge in my gut. I *knew* something about this kid wasn't right. He bit his thumbnail. He was jittery, too nervous for a guy that good-looking.

"Hey," I said, walking over to him. He startled, then immediately darted through the crowd. "Hey, wait!" I called out again.

The kid bolted across the parking lot. A glove dropped from his pocket, landing on the pavement. He paused as if to pick it up but saw me following and took off.

I ran after him, but when I turned the corner, the kid was gone. He had disappeared down one of the many alleys between buildings.

I walked back to the pet-store parking lot. I hoped the guy's girlfriend was still there so I could get his name, but she was gone too.

I paused before picking up the kid's glove. I knew if I touched it, I might have a vision as I had the night before. The feeling wasn't pleasant. The vision had left me dizzy and a little frightened.

Still, I had to know where the kid had gone. He could be the arsonist who had started all those fires. I picked up the glove and held it in both hands.

All at once the vision hit me. I was *there*, standing at the back of the feed shed, but the fire hadn't started yet. In my mind, I had returned to the past. I couldn't see much, just a hazy figure. The person held what looked like a jerry can full of gas.

"Claire, are you all right?" As soon as the fire chief took my arm, I was back in the present, in the pet-store parking lot. The burned feed shed smoked as the firefighters mopped up after the fire.

"What was that all about?" Jim asked me.

I was confused a moment, thinking the fire chief was talking about my vision.

"I turned and saw you run off around the corner," he told me.

"Oh, that," I said. "I was chasing after a kid. The guy was nervous, like he was afraid of something. He took off when I tried to talk to him. I think he may be the firebug."

"Do you know who the kid is?"

"No." I looked down at the glove. "Chief, he dropped this. When I picked it up, I had a vision."

"Like the one you had last night about Amber?"

I shook my head. "This one was different. When I had that vision about Amber, I felt like I was with her in the present. This time I had a vision of the past. In it, I saw someone setting that fire."

"The boy you just chased?"

"I was holding the kid's glove when I had it, so I guess it must be him. In the vision, I didn't see the firebug's face. I only saw a guy's back. At least, I think it was a man. He held a jerry can of gas. Like what you'd use to fill a lawn mower."

"We found a jerry can at the other fires. If that kid used gas to start this one, then the jerry can may still be here.

"I imagine."

"Okay, I'll take a look. If I find it, maybe we can pull some fingerprints." The fire chief started to walk back to the smoldering shed.

"Jim, wait." He turned back. "In the vision, I saw the figure at the back of the shed. He was over there, close to those houses."

"Show me."

I led the chief to the back of the blackened building as his team rolled up the hoses. Past the fire scene, there were three sets of boot prints in the snow. Two were men's boot prints and the third belonged to a small woman. The biggest prints led from the burned building to a nearby house.

"Careful not to step on those prints," Jim said. "The cops will want to take a look."

We stepped to the side as we followed the footprints into the backyard of the house. They stopped at a garden shed and then doubled back. Jim opened the shed door. He pulled out a jerry can.

"The firebug must have stolen the gas from here," said Jim. "He's done the same thing in the last four fires. He always puts the jerry can back where he found it. He sets things up so the fire smolders for a while before the flames burn the building."

"So he can leave the building before anyone notices the smoke."

"That's my guess."

"What about those other footprints at the back of the feed shed? Are another man and woman involved?"

"Arsonists usually work alone. Maybe the owners of this place saw something." The chief glanced at the empty driveway and darkened windows of the house. "No one's home now. I'll stop by here later and ask the homeowners a few questions."

"So what do you think? Was the arsonist that kid I saw?"

"Very likely, if he was jumpy enough to run away."

I held out the kid's glove. "Then all I have to do is figure out who this belongs to."

"Yes, but quickly. From what I see here, the firebug is getter bolder and more dangerous. He'll likely set another building on fire here, in town."

"We've got to stop him before he burns down a place with people in it," I said. "We've got to stop him before he kills someone."

THREE

I wasn't going to let this firebug get away. The kid had run off on foot. He couldn't have gotten far. I started up my car and headed in the direction he'd gone.

I drove slowly, peering down each alley. Businesses were starting to open. I passed Tommy's Café and saw Matt's car parked in front. I guess he'd gone back in for coffee after dropping mine off at the newspaper office.

I inched along, checking street after street. Then I circled my car around again. Nothing. Yet the kid had to be here some- where. Maybe he lived downtown, in one of the apartments above the businesses. But which one?

After a good hour of searching, I finally parked my car in front of Tommy's Café next to Matt's. I held the kid's glove, hoping for a vision. Maybe I could pick up on where the kid was. I had used Amber's bracelet to find her the night before.

I willed a vision to come and got nothing. Then I remembered what Mom had told me. I had to relax in order to see where the person was. Mom said I should meditate on the object. I had to clear my mind and let the vision come to me. I couldn't force it.

Still holding the glove, I closed my eyes and took deep breaths. After a few minutes, I felt my body relax and my mind calm.

Just when I thought I might get a vision, I heard a knock on my window. I opened my eyes. Matt waved at me from outside the passenger door. Shit, I thought. He had caught me meditating in my car. He would think I was as odd as my mother.

I rolled down the window and tried my best to smile back.

"Are you on a stakeout?" he asked. He laughed. "Spying on some criminal?"

"Something like that," I said. I didn't laugh with him. Lack of sleep had made me cranky. I didn't feel like being the butt of jokes this early in the morning.

Matt thumbed Tommy's Café. I looked over my shoulder to see Fire Chief Wallis and his crew sitting at the counter in front of the café window. Jim gave me a little wave and laughed with one of the men, clearly at my expense. He must have taken the firefighters out for breakfast after the fire. I just hoped Trevor wasn't there to see me with Matt.

"The boys are ribbing me for keeping you out all night," said Matt. "They think you fell asleep in the car."

"If you must know, I'm meditating."

"Meditating?"

"Jim may have told you I saw a kid at the fire who was acting strange. I think he might be the firebug. He dropped his glove." I held it up. "I was trying to track him with it. I thought maybe holding it would trigger a vision. It did this morning."

"You were trying to have a vision?" Matt held up both hands. "Well, don't let me stop you."

I sighed. "It's okay. I got nothing."

Then, just like that, the vision hit. I felt a rush, like I was zooming down a water-slide tunnel. Then I saw the firebug walking through the alley between the old movie theater and the bank. This time I knew the vision was in the present. How, I don't know. I just *knew*.

"Are you okay?" said Matt. "You looked like you were about to faint."

As soon as I heard Matt speak, I startled back to myself. "The kid who owns this glove is here, close by," I told him. "By the old theater. Matt, I'm sure he's the firebug."

"Okay, let's go."

That felt good. I didn't have to fight Matt to get him to believe me. He understood I really could find people with my visions. I had proven myself the night before—to him, at least.

I got out of the car and led the way. The theater was only a block from where I had parked my car. What I saw in my vision was real. The kid was there, crossing the street. His red-haired girlfriend was walking with him.

"Hey!" I shouted.

The kid turned, saw me and bolted. The girl ran off in the opposite direction.

"That's him," I exclaimed. "You've got to catch him." I knew there was no way I could outrun the kid. He had the build of a jock.

"Wait here," Matt said. He sprinted down the snowy sidewalk after the boy. Matt was a jogger. Within moments he'd tackled the kid, pressing him to the ground.

I watched as Matt hauled the firebug up by his coat collar. He walked the guy down the street toward me. The kid looked scared out of his wits.

Matt, on the other hand, appeared worried. "Are you sure about this?" he asked me as he approached.

"I'm positive," I said.

"Okay, your call."

"We should let the chief handle it," I said. "Let him question the kid."

"You got it."

Matt dragged the firebug into Tommy's Café, and I followed. Trevor *was* there, sitting at a table to the side with some of the other firefighters. Some of the cops were also there for a coffee break.

"What do we have here?" Jim asked. He turned to the firebug. "Devon, what's going on?" I was surprised the fire chief knew the boy. Matt let the kid go.

"We caught your arsonist," I said. I waved a hand at the boy, Devon. I felt pretty darn proud of myself in that moment. My vision had solved yet another crime. I was on a roll.

Jim glanced around the café, at everyone watching. "Claire," he said to me, "this isn't the place for this." He pulled Devon outside. Matt and I followed. I was surprised when Trevor did too.

"Got anything to say for yourself, son?" the fire chief asked the kid. "*Did* you start those fires?"

Devon shook his head. But he also looked at his feet, like he had something to hide.

Trevor took my arm so I would face him. "What's all this about?" he asked. He was still sooty from the fire. That just seemed to make him more handsome.

"I tracked down the firebug," I told him. I nodded at Devon.

"You think Devon is the arsonist?" Trevor asked. He looked at Devon and shook his head. "I don't think so."

At that moment I saw Devon's red-haired girlfriend walk by on the opposite side of the street. Trevor's face clouded when he saw her. He clearly didn't like the girl. She paused and walked on.

"It's true," I told Trevor. "I saw Devon in a vision, setting the fire. He was also acting suspiciously at the fire scene. He ran when I tried to confront him."

"And he ran just now," Matt said, supporting me. "When we tried to stop him."

Trevor eyed Matt and then squeezed my arm a little too hard. "Claire, I know Devon didn't set that fire."

"I know he did," I said. "I saw him."

"In a vision."

I hesitated. Everyone inside the café was watching us. They all knew my mother and her nutty ways. I knew how they would see me.

"Yes," I said finally. "I saw Devon start that fire in a vision." At least, I thought I had. Now I was beginning to doubt myself.

"No, you didn't," said Trevor.

"How could you possibly know what I saw?"

Trevor glanced back at the café. Then he looked down at me. "Claire, I know you didn't see Devon start that fire because Devon is my brother."

FOUR

I looked up at Trevor, shocked. "Your brother?" I said. "The firebug is your brother?"

"He's no arsonist, but yes, Devon is my brother."

I studied Devon's handsome face. Now that I knew he was Trevor's brother, I could see they were family. Devon did look a lot like his older brother, though he hadn't filled out yet. He was still on the skinny side.

"I thought you knew," said Matt. "You were dating Trevor. That's why I asked if you were sure about this."

"I've never met Trevor's family," I told him.

"I'm not a firebug," Devon said. "I've never set a fire in my life." He looked up as he thought that one through. "Well, maybe a campfire. But I've never set a building on fire."

"So why did you run from the parking lot?" I asked him. "Why did you leave your glove behind?"

"I was late for class," he said. "At the college."

I wasn't convinced. "Why were you at the fire in the first place?" I asked.

Trevor answered for him. "Devon tries to make it to all the fires," he said. "To watch and learn. He wants to be a fire-fighter, just like me." He stood straighter when he said that. He could have burst a button on his shirt, he was so proud. Obviously, the two brothers were close.

The chief put a hand on my shoulder. "Look, Claire, I know Devon. He's a good kid. He's no firebug. Unless you've got some kind of proof, I've got to put a stop to this."

"When I picked up his glove, I saw the arsonist set that fire."

"I know. And I know your mother really believes in her visions. But Claire, her visions are so often wrong. Maybe yours was too?"

"My vision led me to find Amber Miller last night."

"I know, I know. I'm just saying, we can't go around accusing people of arson based on your visions." He glanced back at the others, watching from their tables inside the café. "Especially not in public. Claire, you've got to be careful here. You'll end up with a reputation like your mother's."

I knew he was right. Almost everyone in this logging town figured my mother was a nutcase. She ran yoga classes and drank herbal tea, for god's sake.

"I get it," I said. "You're right. I'm sorry. I guess I'm not thinking straight. I didn't get much sleep last night."

"How about you go home and grab a nap? I'll take it from here."

I nodded, defeated. I felt like a child, surrounded by all these big, burly fire-fighters.

"I'm so sorry," I told Trevor.

"I'm not the one you should be apologizing to," he said.

"You're right, of course," I said. I turned to his brother. "Devon, this is all my fault. Matt had nothing to do with it. I told him to grab you."

"It's okay," Devon mumbled. He glanced at Trevor and away, as if embarrassed that his brother was there. I felt like a real shit

34

then. I had humiliated the poor kid in front of his big brother.

I turned back to Trevor. "I hope this doesn't sour things between us. Friends?"

"More than friends," he said, taking my hand. "How about dinner tomorrow night?"

Matt stepped forward. "We have plans," he told Trevor. I heard the warning in Matt's voice. Matt had asked me out to dinner, and I had said yes.

"Maybe another time?" I said hopefully.

"Come on," Matt said. He took my other hand and pulled me to his truck. "I'll give you a lift home. You're so tired you're acting like a drunk. You shouldn't be driving."

He was right. I *was* acting as reckless as a drunk. Here I was, trying to make dinner plans with Trevor in front of Matt.

I glanced back at Devon before getting in the truck. He held my gaze a moment, then looked away.

I felt that familiar ache in my gut. Something wasn't right. I *knew* that kid was hiding something. I couldn't let this go. If Devon was the firebug like I thought, I needed to find proof.

Once we reached my building, Matt walked me to my apartment door. There, he gave me a peck on the cheek. That was a first. He hadn't kissed me the night before.

"Get some sleep," he told me. "See you tomorrow night? I'll pick you up at seven."

"Yes, tomorrow."

I watched him stride down the hall. Matt was practical and steady, the kind of man a girl could marry. Trevor on the other hand? Well, Trevor was eye candy. He was yummy. I wasn't sure I was ready for the marrying kind.

I unlocked my door and went inside. I had a bachelor apartment, just big enough for me and my few things. I'd done my best to liven the place up, but it still looked lonely when I walked in.

The cupboards of the kitchen were old and dark. My small couch and oversized television filled my tiny living room. My tropical plants needed watering. They drooped.

I threw my keys on the kitchen table and grabbed my cell. I needed sleep, but I had to phone Mom to make sure she was okay first. I had put her through hell the night before. I had dragged her up a snowy mountain to find Amber.

The phone rang several times before Mom picked up on her end. When she did, her voice sounded groggy. "Hello?"

"I woke you, didn't I?"

"We were up so late." She yawned. "I expect you were up much later."

"Yeah, I didn't get much sleep."

Her voice brightened. "Oh! So I guess your date went well."

"My date with Trevor? I missed it to find Amber, remember?"

"I meant your date with Matt. You were off to have a burger when I left the search-and-rescue camp."

"Oh, Matt. Yes, that was nice. We talked well into the night."

"You just *talked*?"

"Mom!"

"I do want grandchildren, you know."

"As you keep telling me," I said.

"Well, maybe you'll do more than talk next time."

"I don't know. We'll see. Trevor turned up at my office this morning."

"Mad, I bet."

"Yeah, but he still wants to see me. And then at the fire—"

"Fire, what fire?"

"At the garden and pet store," I told her. "The feed shed burned down this morning. The chief thinks an arsonist set it on fire."

"The chief? How is he? I've been meaning to call. I've been thinking a lot about him lately."

"Mom. Focus. I was telling you about Trevor."

"Oh, yes, of course. Trevor. The hunky firefighter."

"Yes, at the fire he was so, so…"

"Manly."

"Yes!" I said. "He was so strong, so sure of himself. I loved watching him put out that fire."

"Aha."

"What do you mean, *aha*?"

"Now that Matt is interested, you suddenly want to see Trevor again."

"I didn't say that."

"You didn't have to. It's one man or the other, my girl."

"Does it have to be?" I asked. "Why can't I date two men at once? Men go out with more than one woman all the time."

"And how would you feel if your date went out with another woman? Really, Claire. Try that and you'll end up alone."

"I'm a big girl, Mom. I'll be thirty-one next spring. You don't need to give me dating advice."

"You're playing with fire," she told me.

"Maybe," I said. I was too tired to argue. I said my goodbye, lay back on the couch and fell fast asleep.

FIVE

I woke to the smell of smoke. Fire! I sat up, confused. What time was it? Why was I sleeping on the couch?

My cell read *8:30*, but it was dark outside. It was eight thirty at night. I had slept through the whole day. How could I have slept the whole day?

Then I remembered. I hadn't got much sleep the night before. Then there was the fire at the pet store that morning. I had a vision of the firebug. Then Matt and I had chased after Devon. Crap!

I held my head in both hands. I had made a fool of myself in front of the fire chief and Trevor. What kind of reporter was I? I had been trained to make sure I got the facts of my story right before printing it. And yet I'd accused Trevor's brother of arson without any proof whatsoever.

I stood and shook myself fully awake. Yes, I could definitely smell smoke. The wail of the alarm at the firehouse sounded. I looked out the window. Smoke billowed from the center of town. I felt that tug in my gut. Shit. The firebug had struck again. I *knew* it.

I texted my editor. The fire. On it! Then I threw on my winter jacket and grabbed my car keys from the kitchen table. Matt had driven me home that morning. My car was still at Tommy's Café. I would just have to hoof it.

I ran down the steps of my apartment building. Fortunately, I didn't live far from the town center. I jogged quickly down the snowy street, careful not to slip on the icy sidewalk. When I reached my car, I grabbed my camera from the front seat.

I could see the smoke billowing above the town center. The post office was there. The cop shop, firehall and movie theater were all in that downtown core. The glow of a fire colored the clouds over the town red.

I turned the corner and saw the blaze. Fire Chief Wallis and his team were already at work trying to put out the flames. The lumber shed behind the hardware store was on fire. The whole building was consumed in smoke and flames. To the side of the fire, there was a jerry can of gas.

When the chief stepped back to watch his team, I moved forward to talk to him. "The arsonist struck again?" I asked Jim.

"This time the firebug didn't try to hide the jerry can," he told me. "He's getting brazen, careless."

"It seems odd, though, doesn't it? Why would the firebug just leave the jerry can out like that?"

"Who knows? Maybe he heard someone coming and fled."

"But you said he's been so careful at the other fires. He didn't leave any evidence behind."

"He left no fingerprints on the jerry can at the pet-store fire this morning. We haven't found fingerprints at any of the fires. But maybe he didn't have time to wipe his fingerprints off that jerry can this time."

One of the firefighters waved Jim over. "Got to go," Jim told me. He went back to the fire to instruct a member of his team.

I watched Trevor handle the hose. He leaned back, using the power of his own body to direct the spray of water. Winter was on us, but he was sweating with the effort. He had never looked so good.

I took a few shots of him with my camera. Then I scanned the crowd that watched the fire, looking for Devon. If he was the firebug, I figured he'd be here. I didn't see Devon, but I did see his girlfriend. Her dyed red hair made her stand out in the crowd. She wore a green winter coat that showed off that hair even more.

"Hey," I called. "I need to talk to you."

When she saw me, she looked scared. She immediately turned and pushed her way through the crowd.

"Wait!" I called out after her. "I just want to ask you some questions." Then, to the crowd, I said, "Somebody stop her!"

A middle-aged man stood in her way. The girl stopped just long enough for me to grab her arm.

As soon as I touched the girl's sleeve, I had a vision of the immediate past. I saw this girl here at this fire, before anyone arrived. She held that jerry can of gas.

In front of her, the fire had only just started. This girl had started the fire!

Shocked, I let go of the girl's sleeve, and the vision dissolved. I was back in the present. The crowd milled around me. The girl, caught, turned to look at me.

"You started that fire," I said.

"No, I—" she stuttered. "You don't understand."

"I understand someone could have been killed. That fire could have spread to the hardware store. You're lucky the staff wasn't working late in that warehouse."

"I didn't start the fire."

"Then why did you run just now?"

She didn't answer.

"What's your name?"

She paused before answering. "Kayla. Kayla Porter."

"You're Devon's girlfriend?"

"Yes."

"Are you two starting these fires together?"

"No!"

"But I saw both of you at these fires." I neglected to tell her I had seen her and Devon at the fires in my *visions*.

Jim Wallis strode toward us in full firefighting gear. "What's going on?" he asked. The fire chief was clearly nervous about me causing trouble again. He must have seen me run after Kayla.

"Chief, I saw her set that fire," I told him. "I saw her standing right there with a jerry can in her hand. The building was on fire."

"You saw this with your own eyes?" he asked. "Or did you see this in one of your visions?"

"I saw it with my own eyes." I paused. "In a vision."

The chief nodded slowly, as if figuring out what to say next. He clearly didn't believe me. "Claire, we've had this discussion. First you say Devon is the firebug. Now you say

Kayla is the arsonist. Making false accusations of this kind is very serious." He glanced at the crowd around us. "You could get yourself in real trouble."

"I know," I said. "But I also know what I saw. We can't let this girl start another fire. She's targeting businesses now. Imagine if she hits a shed behind a grocery or restaurant next. People could die."

"You don't have to lecture me about the dangers of arson," the chief said.

I looked down, feeling stupid.

"You're really sure about this, aren't you?" Jim asked me.

"Yes, I'm sure. I saw her holding that jerry can."

He watched me for a moment. I could see him trying to make up his mind whether to believe me or not. "All right," he said. He took Kayla by the arm. "I'll have her taken in for questioning. If her fingerprints are on that jerry can, then we have a case against her."

"No, wait!" Devon called.

We all turned. Devon jogged toward us in a hoodie, not a winter coat, even though the night was cold.

So, I thought, Devon had been here at the fire all along. Had he been hiding in the alley nearby, peering around the corner?

"You've got it all wrong," Devon told me. "Kayla didn't set that fire. You can't take her in."

"What do you mean?" the chief asked Devon. "What's going on?"

Devon took a deep breath to steady himself. "Claire was right this morning. I set that fire. I'm the firebug."

SIX

The fire chief looked stricken. Clearly, he liked Devon and was shocked the kid had confessed. So I was right. Devon *was* the firebug.

"Oh, Devon," Jim said. "Tell me this is some kind of sick joke." I suddenly realized the chief had been grooming Devon. He had wanted the kid to be part of his firefighting team. No chance of that now, I thought.

"No joke," said Devon. He lifted his chin to the fire behind us. "I set that fire.

I set all those shed fires—by myself. Just leave Kayla out of this, okay?"

"But she was here when you set that fire, wasn't she?" I asked. "I saw her holding the jerry can," I told him.

"In your vision," the chief corrected me.

I looked around at the crowd. Most were watching the fire, but those closest to us were listening to our conversation. I lowered my voice, hoping they wouldn't hear. "In my vision," I told Jim.

"Kayla had nothing to do with this," Devon told me. "I set those fires."

Kayla put a hand on Devon's arm. "Devon, no."

"I won't let you take the heat for this," he told her.

At least the kid was taking responsibility, I thought.

Kayla shook her head. Her red hair swirled around her face. She looked miserable.

"But why?" the chief asked Devon. "Why did you set all those fires?"

"I don't know."

"You burn all these buildings and that's all you've got to say? I don't know?"

Devon looked to the ground to avoid the chief's angry gaze.

"I wish I knew," he said.

"All right," said the chief, shaking his head. "I'll hand you over to the cops. You can explain all this to them. I don't need to tell you how disappointed I am in you. At least you won't set another fire. You're lucky no one got hurt. If someone had been killed in one of these fires, you'd be facing a murder charge."

The police arrived within minutes. I stood back, taking notes, as the cops asked their questions of both Devon and the chief. They questioned Kayla, but they didn't talk to me. The fire chief didn't direct the cops my way. He didn't tell them that my vision had led to Devon's arrest.

I figured Jim was protecting me in his way. He knew the cops thought my mom was nuts for telling them she had visions. The chief cared about both Mom and me. He didn't want to see my reputation damaged further.

I glanced over at Trevor. He was busy fighting the fire and had no idea his brother was being arrested for arson. What was he going to think of me when he found out? My accusation that Kayla had started those fires had led to Devon's arrest.

The crowd watching the fire clapped as Trevor put out the last of the flames. Then the chief waved him over. Jim told him about Devon, and Trevor sprinted to the cop car, horrified. He spoke to his brother through the closed window. "Devon, no! What are you doing?

Trevor stood to face Jim. "Chief, you know Devon would never do this. He wants to be a firefighter. He's a good kid."

"I can't believe it either," said the chief. "But he just admitted he started those fires. He gave me a full confession."

Trevor put a hand to the window separating them. "We'll figure this out," he told his brother. "You're not in this alone."

But Devon wouldn't look at his brother. His face reddened in shame.

Trevor and I watched as the cops drove him away.

I took Trevor's sooty hand. "Trevor, I'm so sorry," I told him. "I saw Kayla with the jerry can in another vision. I told the chief. Devon confessed then."

"Why would he do that? This is so messed up."

Trevor was understandably upset, but something about his reaction didn't feel right. "Trevor, is there something you're not telling me?" I asked him. "Did you know Devon was setting fires?"

Trevor let go of my hand. "No, of course not. I had no idea he started those fires. I don't believe he really did." He took off his helmet and ran a hand through his hair. "I'm sorry you found yourself in the middle of this. I hope what happened doesn't change things between us."

"No, of course not," I said. "How could it? Your brother's actions aren't your responsibility."

Trevor watched the cop car turn the corner, heading to the station. "Maybe. Maybe they are."

"You can't take this on yourself," the chief told Trevor. "Devon is nineteen. He's an adult now. He knew what he was doing."

Trevor looked so deflated standing there with his helmet in his hand. I thought he might cry. I didn't want to see a fire-fighter cry. That just wouldn't be right. It would be like seeing Superman having a meltdown.

"Listen, you were terrific today," I said. "Just now and this morning. Putting out those fires. I love watching you work."

Trevor turned to me and tried to put on a brave face. "More than you like watching Matt work?"

"I have to say you put on more of a show," I said. I returned his smile. "Listen, I'm a little embarrassed by Matt's behavior," I confessed. "It seems he's jealous of you."

"He should be." Trevor pushed my hair from my face. "Don't worry," he said. "I can handle Matt. I like a challenge. Let the better man win. What say we have dinner Thursday night?"

I glanced at the chief, wondering what he thought of us at this moment. It felt strange to have Trevor asking me out on a date under these circumstances. His brother had just been arrested for arson. But then, maybe Trevor felt he needed to talk to someone about it.

"Sure," I said. "I'd like that. Dinner. Thursday."

"It's a date," he said.

SEVEN

Matt opened the door for me as we entered the Lakeshore Bar and Grill. The restaurant was a favorite date spot for couples. Tonight the place was packed.

The hostess led us to our table and left menus with us. Matt held my chair for me as I sat down. "Well, aren't you the gentleman?" I asked him. "I like this side of you."

Matt sat down across from me. "You sound like you haven't seen this side of me before."

"I'm not sure I have," I said. "You've been cranky with me in the past."

Matt's cheeks reddened. I had embarrassed him. I didn't think that was possible.

"I'm sorry about that," he said. "I always found you attractive. I just—"

"You don't like reporters. I know."

"I don't like anyone who pries into other people's lives."

"Speaking of prying," I said, "I'm surprised you still wanted to go out with me tonight."

"What do you mean?"

"I made such a fool of myself at Tommy's Café. I accused Devon of arson. Everyone thought I was nuts."

"I'm sure they feel differently now," Matt told me. "You were right. Devon admitted he set those fires."

"Yes, he did."

"You sound doubtful. Is something else going on?"

I shook my head. "It's probably nothing."

"I still can't believe Devon set those fires," Matt said. "I know that kid. He's volunteered on a few searches for lost hikers. He's honest, and he really looks out for people, you know? He's mature for his age." Matt paused, looking at the menu. "More mature than his older brother," he added.

I let that last comment pass. "I can't say Devon seems mature, not if he's setting fires. Someone could have been hurt." I put down my menu. "Still, you're right. Something about his confession feels off."

"I take it you had one of your hunches?"

I shook my head, uncertain. "I don't know. It's like he was covering for someone else."

"His girlfriend?"

"That would be my first guess."

"Well, let's put work aside for tonight, okay? I've been looking forward to this evening all day."

I smiled at Matt. "Me too."

Matt glanced around. "I hope you don't think it's weird that I took you here."

"Weird? How is it weird?"

"You were on your way to a date with Trevor at this restaurant the other night. Then you got that hunch of yours."

"That gut feeling that led me to find Amber Miller."

"And drew us together," he said. He took my hand and held my gaze for a moment. "I tried making a reservation at the Boardwalk Café, but they were booked. This was the only place that still had a table open."

"I like this place," I said. "I'm glad you brought me here."

"Things *are* over between you and Trevor, right?"

I let go of Matt's hand. I took a long drink of water as I thought about how to answer.

"Well?" said Matt. When I paused a moment longer, he said, "You're still seeing him, aren't you?"

I put my glass down. "We're having dinner at the Boardwalk Café tomorrow night."

Matt sat back, clearly pissed. "You're two-timing me?"

"No! It's not like that."

"You're on a date with me tonight and out with Trevor tomorrow night. You're dating two men. I think that's the definition of two-timing."

The guests at the next table turned to watch us. The couple at another table pointed and whispered. I didn't know them, but they likely knew me from my work at the paper. My picture was on the editorial page every week.

"Look, I've only just started dating you," I said. "It's not like we're a couple or anything."

"And you and Trevor are?

I lowered my voice. "No…"

"Not yet."

"What kind of girl do you take me for?"

"You tell me."

We stared each other down for a moment. Then Matt sniffed. He turned toward the window. "What is that?"

"What?"

"I smell smoke."

"Smoke?" All at once I could smell it too. "Maybe they've burned something in the kitchen."

"I don't think so. That's a garbage fire."

Matt stood and strode out the back exit. I followed. Sure enough, the large garbage bin behind the restaurant was on fire. The bin was butted up against the back wall of the restaurant. The flames had already started to spread to the building.

Matt pulled out his cell. "I'll phone 9-1-1."

"I'll get everyone out of the restaurant."

I went back inside and whistled for everyone's attention. The waitresses and the patrons at their tables looked at me like I was a crazy woman. "We've got a fire at the back of the building," I informed them. "Everyone out through the front entrance. Stay calm, people. Move slowly."

The manager cleared his staff from the kitchen. Once I had walked everyone out of the restaurant, I joined Matt back at the fire. It was larger now, and part of the wall of the restaurant was on fire. I heard the fire alarm at the station go off. The chief and the fire trucks would be here within minutes.

A crowd of onlookers gathered. Then I saw Trevor. He walked down the alley toward us dressed casually, in a winter jacket over jeans and a T-shirt.

"Trevor, what are you doing here? Why aren't you in your firefighting gear?"

"I just happened to be driving by," he said. "I saw the smoke and flames."

He went back into the restaurant and retrieved a couple of fire extinguishers.

As I snapped photos with my cell phone, Trevor quickly used the extinguisher to douse the flames on the building itself. The fire continued to smolder in the metal garbage bin but was no longer a threat to the restaurant. I posted a photo on Twitter with the tweet, Trevor saves the day! The fire trucks arrived, and Trevor helped his team hook up the hoses. They had the fire in the bin completely out within minutes.

Trevor stood back with his arms crossed, looking pretty proud of himself.

"You handled that well," I said.

"It's my job," he told me. "Well, it's my volunteer work. But you know what I mean. I can't let all this training go to waste."

"You say you just happened to be driving by?" Matt asked him. "You weren't checking up on Claire, were you?"

"Why would I do that?"

"You knew she had a date with me tonight."

"Sure, I knew. You told me."

"Matt, this is ridiculous," I said. "Trevor just stopped that fire from spreading to the restaurant. Now you're giving him hell for being here. You're just jealous."

Matt shook his head like he couldn't believe I'd just said that. Then he waved me off, dismissing me. "I'm sure Trevor will be happy to give you a ride home," he said. He turned to leave.

"Matt, wait!" I took his arm. He stopped for a moment but wouldn't look at me.

I glanced at the crowd around us. I knew I would once again be the topic of gossip at Tommy's Café the next day. "I didn't want our time together to end like this," I said.

"Tell that to Trevor."

"Please, Matt. I really like you. I'd like the chance to get to know you better."

He paused. "I'd like that too, Claire. But you've got a choice to make." He lifted his chin at Trevor, watching us from the smoking bin. "It's either him or me."

Matt turned on his heel and marched to his truck. I followed him for a few steps, then gave up. He drove off without looking back.

EIGHT

Trevor caught up with me as I watched Matt drive away. Behind him, the fire chief and his crew cleaned up after the fire.

"Did I just ruin your date?" Trevor asked. He grinned sideways, like he was okay with that.

"No," I said. "Things went sour before you got here."

He held me gently by the shoulders. "I know for a fact we'll have a lot more fun tomorrow night," he told me. He held my gaze to make it clear what he had in mind. I turned away, blushing.

That's when I saw her. The redhead, Devon's girlfriend, watched us from the corner of the next building. Kayla put a finger to her lips, telling me to keep quiet. Then she waved me over. She disappeared behind the building so no one else would see her.

"Trevor," I said. "You mind giving me a minute? I'll be right back."

"Sure," he said. "Where are you going?"

"Following up on a hunch," I told him.

I walked to the next building and looked around. Kayla stood in front of the gas station across the street, hugging herself. She waved me over again.

When I reached her, she looked around nervously. The smoke from the bin fire still hung above the restaurant building. "Did anyone follow you?" she said.

I looked back with her. I couldn't see Trevor or the crowd from where I stood.

The next building was in the way. "No, I don't think so."

"Good."

"Why would anyone follow me?" I asked. "What's going on?" When she didn't answer, I demanded, "What's this about?"

"Devon couldn't have started that fire, could he?" she asked.

"No, he's in custody. The cops locked him up in a cell at the police station."

"So who *did* set it?"

"I don't know." I paused. "Did you?"

"Would I be talking to you, a reporter, if I did?"

"I don't know, Kayla. I did see you holding a jerry can at the last fire."

"In a vision," she said.

"Yes, in a vision. But you are here, at this fire."

"I didn't start this fire," Kayla told me. "I didn't start the fire at the hardware store.

Neither did Devon. He hasn't started any of these fires."

"Then who did?"

"I can't tell you that."

"You can't tell me, or you won't?"

She looked away, caught. "I'm just saying you've got to keep looking into this," she said. "The arsonist is still out there. He'll keep setting fires in town until someone gets hurt."

"You know exactly who started those fires, don't you?"

Kayla bit her thumbnail but didn't answer.

"*Is* it you?"

"No!" Kayla cried. "It's not me and it's not Devon. You can't let him go to prison for this."

"If someone else is responsible for these fires, you need to tell me who he is. If not me, then tell the chief. He cares about Devon."

She shook her head. "The chief would never believe me."

"If you saw someone start a fire, why didn't you use your cell phone to take a photo of him?"

"You don't understand," she said. "I can't be the one—" She didn't finish her sentence. Her attention was caught by something behind me. I looked back. Trevor strode toward us. "I've got to go," said Kayla. With that, she turned and fled.

"Wait!" I tried running after Kayla, but I was wearing heels. She wasn't. I watched her run away down the snowy street.

Trevor caught up to me. "What's going on?"

"I'm not sure. Kayla was just here. She told me Devon didn't set those fires. Then she just ran off."

"You know what I think?" he asked. "You were right about Kayla. She started all these fires, and Devon is covering for her.

"She says someone else is responsible."

"Of course she would say that," said Trevor. "She's lying to protect herself."

"Then why doesn't she just let Devon take the blame?"

Trevor shrugged. "They've been dating for a while. She must care for him. I suppose she doesn't want to see him hurt."

"I don't know," I said. My instincts told me there was more going on. But what?

Trevor and I walked back to the restaurant and watched the firefighters roll up the hoses. Fire Chief Wallis joined us. "This fire was definitely arson," Jim said. "I thought we'd licked this thing."

"Well, we know Devon didn't start *this* fire," Trevor said to him. "He's in custody."

"Must be a copycat arsonist," the chief said. "Some other kid is starting fires now."

"I don't think so," Trevor said. "I know Devon didn't start those other fires. I don't care what he says. He's covering for someone.

Someone *close*." He let his accusation hang there.

"His girlfriend, Kayla?" Jim asked.

"I just saw Kayla over at the gas station," I told the chief. "She claims someone else is responsible."

Trevor shook his head. "No. I'm sure Kayla started those fires. She was here tonight, wasn't she?"

"Kayla's fingerprints *were* on that jerry can at the hardware store," Jim said.

"I'm betting Devon's fingerprints were *not* on that gas can," Trevor said.

The chief looked surprised. "How did you know?"

"I asked around today," Trevor said. "The manager at the hardware store said he saw Devon running down the street toward the fire *after* our trucks got there."

"That doesn't prove anything," said the chief. "He could have set the fire and left, to avoid suspicion. Then he came back to watch the fire. The firebug has done just that at each of these fires."

"I *know* Devon would never start a fire like that. Like I said, he's trying to protect Kayla."

Jim took off his firefighter's helmet. "Trevor, I don't want to believe Devon did this any more than you do. But he admitted to starting the fires." He turned to me. "And you said you saw him at those fires in your visions."

"I know. But now I'm not so sure he started them."

"You said you saw Kayla in your last vision," said Trevor. "You said she started the fire, remember?"

"I only saw her holding that jerry can."

"I *know* Devon is covering for some-one," said Trevor. "And like you said, Kayla's fingerprints are on that jerry can, not Devon's."

"Maybe the firebug isn't either of them," I said. "Maybe the arsonist is someone else entirely."

Jim looked fed up with me. "You hold Devon's glove and get a vision," he told me. "You're sure he started the fire. Then you get another vision and you're sure Kayla is the arsonist. Now you think the firebug is someone else? Who?"

"I don't know," I said.

"Well, when you figure it out, you let me know. I don't want to see an innocent kid go to jail. Especially a great kid like Devon."

I looked up at Trevor. "Me neither," I said. "I feel responsible for this mess. I've got to find a way to prove Devon is innocent."

"How, exactly?" said Trevor. "With your visions?" His impatience stung me, but I let it go. I imagined he was much more worried about Devon than he let on.

"Maybe," I said. In my visions, I had only seen bits and pieces of what happened. Clearly, I didn't understand what I had seen. I knew only one person who had the experience to help me sort this all out.

NINE

Mom's driveway was full of cars the next morning. I knew she was teaching yoga, so I didn't bother to knock. She wouldn't answer the door when she had a class in session.

As soon as I stepped into her kitchen, I was greeted by soothing music. Her living room was filled with seniors standing on their yoga mats. All of them were touching their toes in the same yoga pose.

"Claire!" Mom said when I entered the room. She was still bent over. "What are you doing here?" Her face looked strange upside down.

I turned my head to look at her. "Um, can we talk?"

"I'm kind of in the middle of something," she said.

I pointed a thumb at the kitchen, trying to get her to come with me. "It's important," I said.

Mom slowly rose and held out both arms in Warrior pose. The elderly women all followed her lead. "We can talk now," Mom said.

"I need to talk to you *alone*," I said.

"We're all friends here, aren't we, ladies?"

The seniors murmured in agreement and switched poses on Mom's cue. All of them wore snazzy yoga outfits. Mom's was black and yellow. She looked a little like a bumblebee.

"But it's about that thing we do," I whispered. I waved a hand in a circle. "You know, the *thing*." I meant the premonitions both Mom and I had—our second sight.

Mom got it. "The ladies know about our visions, dear," she said.

"They do?" I scanned the group. "You *told* them?"

"It's all right," Mom said. "You can talk freely."

I shook my head at my own attempt to hide my "secret." What did it matter? The whole town knew about my visions now.

"I've been working with the fire chief on that string of fires," I told Mom. "We've been trying to track down the arsonist."

"Oh, good for you!" Mom said. "Somebody has to catch that kid before anyone gets hurt."

"A boy was arrested for setting the fires."

"So what's the problem?" Mom asked me.

"My visions are giving me mixed messages about who the firebug is. One minute they tell me one thing. The next, they tell me something else."

"Your hunches and those visions can only point you in a direction," she said. "You still have to figure things out for yourself."

"I know," I said. I'd learned that one the hard way.

"It's so easy to misinterpret what you see in those visions," she said. "I often completely misunderstand the images I see."

"I sure know about that," I said. "I thought I saw Devon setting those fires. Then I thought I saw Kayla. Now I'm not sure it was either of them."

I rubbed my forehead with the palm of my hand. "What good are these visions if they leave me so damn confused?"

"We often have trouble seeing what's right in front of us," said Mom. "I had no idea your father was having an affair with that waitress at Tommy's Café. I picked up his socks from the floor every day, and I never once had a vision of him with that woman."

"I'm not sure what you're getting at," I said.

"Have you chosen yet?"

"You mean, have I decided who the firebug is?"

"No, between Matt and Trevor. Have you chosen your man?"

"I had dinner with Matt last night," I said. "Well, at least until the garbage bin behind the restaurant caught on fire." I brightened. "I'm having dinner with Trevor tonight."

"You're going to lose them both," Mom warned.

"I'm just dating them," I said, "trying them on for size."

"Matt and Trevor are men, not shoes," Mom scolded. "You don't need to try them on."

"Okay, okay, I'll make a choice," I said. "*After* I catch this firebug."

"I just hope that's not too late," Mom warned me. "Matt is a good catch."

"So is Trevor."

Mom grunted. Obviously, she had made her choice for me. She liked Matt, not Trevor. Her opinion made me want to date Trevor even more.

"I should get going," I said. "Sorry to interrupt your class." I turned to leave.

"Claire," Mom said, stopping me. I looked back. "Sounds like you have two people who do know who that firebug is."

"I already talked to Devon's girlfriend, Kayla. She won't tell me who the arsonist is even to save Devon from jail."

"Then perhaps you need to talk to Devon."

TEN

I went to the police station every morning to pick up the report on crimes from the night before, if there were any. I used that to write stories about break-ins and thefts. So I knew all the police officers. It didn't take much convincing for them to give me a few minutes with Devon.

Devon sat on the top bunk of his cell. I watched Officer Banks slide the cell door closed behind me. I looked around and tried not to touch anything. The bottom mattress of the bunk appeared deeply stained. The cell smelled like puke.

"What are you doing here?" Devon asked.

"My question is, what are you doing here?"

"I think you know the answer to that." He was pissed with me. I was the one who had accused Kayla of arson and forced him to confess.

"I want to know who really set those fires," I said.

"Me," said Devon. But he wouldn't look me in the eye as he said it. I knew he was lying.

"Devon, I think you're covering for someone." I paused, trying to word things carefully. The chief was right. I couldn't go around making accusations anymore, not until I had proof. Still, maybe if I got Devon mad, he'd spill something. "I saw Kayla at the bin fire behind the restaurant," I told him.

"Kayla didn't start that fire!" Devon said. "I keep telling you. I swear, it wasn't Kayla.

She would never set fires. She's, like, all about volunteering. She works at the animal shelter."

I held out both hands. "Okay, okay," I said. "But it wasn't you either, was it? You didn't set those fires."

Devon hung his head but didn't answer.

"The question is, who did? And why would you take the heat for something you didn't do?"

"Maybe I have my reasons." He looked back down, at his feet.

All at once, I understood what was going on. I had held Devon's glove when I first got a vision of the arsonist starting the fire. Devon had been there. I had seen Kayla with the jerry can. She had been there too. But now I understood *why* they had both been there. It wasn't to start the fire. They were trying to stop it.

Like Mom said, so often you can't see what's right in front of you.

I called for one of the cops to let me out of the cell. Then I turned to Devon before leaving. "I got you into this," I said. "I'm going to get you out."

※ ※ ※

My first stop was Tommy's Café. The chief was there with a couple of the volunteer firefighters.

"Hey Claire," he said. "What's up?"

I paused, unsure what to tell the chief. "I know for certain Devon and Kayla didn't start those fires," I said.

"Got proof?"

"No."

"Got some idea who *did* start them?"

I did, but I wouldn't name him. Not yet. "I assume that if I were to get a photo of the firebug setting a fire, you would believe me."

"Of course," Jim said.

"Then that's what I'll do. I'll catch the arsonist in the act."

"How will you know where he's going to set the next fire, or when?" Jim asked. "Did you see something in your visions?" He paused. "You're not seeing into the future now, are you?"

One of the other firefighters, Bruce, smirked. "You start seeing the future, you give me some lottery numbers to play," he said. The other men laughed. I was sure that wasn't the first joke they had told at my expense.

I shook my head. "I didn't get anything useful from my visions," I said. "I'm not sure when or where the firebug will strike next. But I do think I know someone who does."

At noon, I figured I'd find Kayla at Munchies, a coffee shop. It was a local hangout for college kids. I was right. She was in the lineup, waiting for her coffee. She backed away when she saw me, like she was about to bolt again. But I was standing in front of the door.

I held out my hand to calm her. "Kayla," I said, "I've just come to talk."

She looked around at her friends. "Not here," she said.

"No, not here." I waved her outside. "Come on."

Once we were on the sidewalk, she eyed me suspiciously. "What do you want?"

"Look, I know who really started all those fires," I told her.

Her eyes lit up, hopeful. "For real?"

"I know you and Devon were at those fires to stop him. You've both been watching him, haven't you? You've been trying to protect the town. I also know why you both ran when I tried to question you. You've been trying to protect the firebug too."

Kayla looked down. I thought she might cry. "Yes. At first, we didn't want to tell anyone. We thought we could stop him. Then, when he started setting fires in town, we knew no one would believe us." She looked up. "But they might believe you."

I looked around at the shoppers passing by and lowered my voice. "The thing is, I can't point the finger until I have proof."

"Like you accused Devon and me without proof?" She was angry with me. She had every right to be.

"I'm so sorry about that," I said. "I've learned my lesson. I'm trying to set things right. But I need your help."

"I can't testify," she said. "Please don't make me go to court. No one would believe me anyway."

"I know," I said. "Everyone would think you were desperate, trying to clear Devon's name. No one would believe me either. We need to catch the firebug in the act."

"So what do we do?"

I paused. "I need to take a picture of him starting a fire. But to do that, I've got to figure out where he'll hit next, and when. You've been watching the arsonist. You know his habits."

"He starts fires in sheds, outbuildings," she told me. "Places where he thinks no one will get hurt."

"Until he started setting fires in town."

"Yes." She paused. "It's like he was getting bored. He wanted bigger fires. Fires that were harder to put out."

"Fires in public places."

"He wants an audience," said Kayla. "He gets a kick out of people watching." She paused to look at me. "He likes to read about the fires he starts in the news-paper and on Twitter."

A light went on for me then. "You mean, he likes me taking photos at the fire." I felt a chill. "He wants me there."

"Yes."

"Then I know where he's going to strike next."

"How can I help? What do you want me to do?"

"What you always do," I said. "Try to stop him." I looked at my watch. "I have a date with Trevor at the Boardwalk Café at six. Meet me there at five thirty. We'll take it from there."

"Claire?"

I turned back. Kayla looked like she was about to cry. "I don't want to do this," she said.

"Believe me," I said, "neither do I."

ELEVEN

At five thirty I arrived at the Boardwalk Café. I parked my car at the front of the restaurant and got out. Kayla waited for me in her green winter coat. "So what's the plan?" she asked me.

"We go around back," I said. "No one can see the back of the café from the road."

"And if he's there?"

I held up my camera. "I get my photographs and phone the fire chief." I zipped my jacket against the cold. "Let's get this over with."

We circled the restaurant to the alley behind it. I held up my hand to stop Kayla and peeked around the corner. "Shit," I said. "There he is."

Trevor bashed the side of the building with an ax. He stuffed the hole with newspaper and dowsed the paper with gas from a jerry can. He wore gloves so he wouldn't leave fingerprints. Trevor was the firebug. Even as I watched him preparing to start that fire, I didn't want to believe it.

"He's not just messing around with the garbage bin this time," I told Kayla. "He really means to burn this place."

"There are people in there," said Kayla.

"I know. We've got to get a fire truck here, now." I pulled out my cell and phoned the chief. "I've caught the firebug," I told him.

"Who?" he asked.

"You have to see it to believe it." I said Then I described to him where we were. "Come quickly. He's about to start the fire."

"You said you want me to try to stop him," Kayla said when I finished the call.

"I have to get a clear photo of him starting that fire. Talk to him. Get him to look in my direction. I can't face him directly. If he sees me, he may try to stop me from taking pictures."

"Okay, I can do this." Kayla took a deep breath and turned the corner to confront Trevor. I aimed the camera around the edge of the building, hiding as I took photo after photo. With Kayla distracting him, I hoped Trevor wouldn't see me until I got my clear shot.

"Trevor," Kayla called. "Don't."

Trevor heard her. Even so, he struck a match and threw it into the paper before he turned. Fueled by gas, the flames burst to life behind him. "I knew you'd try to stop me again," he told Kayla. "I was counting on it, in fact."

"What are you talking about?" said Kayla.

"I won't let Devon take the rap for this."

"You're trying to frame me."

"You shouldn't have tried to take the jerry can from me at the hardware store. Your fingerprints were all over it. Now I'll tell the chief I saw you starting this fire."

"You won't get away with this."

"Who do you think the cops are going to believe? A teen with fake red hair or a firefighter?"

"They'll believe me," I said. I stepped forward and held up my camera. "Or more to the point, they'll believe what they see with their own eyes. I just took photos of you setting that fire."

"Claire! What are you doing here?"

"We had a date, remember? The question is, what are *you* doing?" The fire now licked the wall. "Trevor, why?" I asked. "Why you, of all people?"

He put out his hand, defending himself. "This isn't what it looks like."

"I confronted Devon," I told him. "He confirmed my suspicions that you've been setting these fires."

"Devon told you that?" Trevor looked stricken for a moment, then straightened. "He's confused. He doesn't know what he's talking about."

"He didn't point the finger at you," I said. "He was ready to go to jail for you. But he told me enough that I figured it out."

"Devon thought if he took the heat for the fires, you would come clean," said Kayla. "He was sure you would admit to setting the fires, to save him from going to jail. Looks like he was wrong."

I held up my camera. "He won't be charged now," I said. "I have proof that you did it."

Trevor took a swift step forward and made a swipe for my camera. "Give me that!"

I ducked out of his way. "It's no use, Trevor," I told him. "I already emailed several photos to my editor. It's over."

In the near distance, the fire truck howled. The chief and his team of fire-fighters were on their way. The scream of the siren seemed to take the fight out of Trevor. He slumped, looking at his large feet like a kid who knew he'd be grounded.

"I just want to understand why you did it," I said. "Why did you set all those fires?"

Trevor stared at the fire a moment before trying to explain himself. "The sheds were all buildings that should have been torn down and burned anyway. At first I was testing my skills. Proving myself."

"At *first*," I said.

"Then…I don't know. Things got out of hand."

"You liked the attention," I said.

He looked up at me. "Yes," he said, as if he only just understood this about himself.

"When the crowd clapped for me at the pet-store fire, I felt great. I liked the way you looked at me then. A celebrity thought I was the hero."

"A celebrity?" I said. I didn't think of myself like that.

"Everyone knows you. You're a *reporter*."

His comment hit like a fist to the stomach. He hadn't gone out with me because he liked *me*. He dated me because he thought I was a local celebrity. I guess I deserved that. I had dated him because he was a firefighter.

"So *you* set the fire in that garbage bin, when I was on my date with Matt."

"I wanted to break up your date. I knew I was losing you to him."

I couldn't believe what I was hearing. "You set this fire so you could be the hero again—on our date."

"And so you'd see Kayla here and think she was the firebug. Like I said, I knew she'd try to stop me. She always does."

"What scares me most is that your plan almost worked," I told him.

"Devon and I used to look up to you," Kayla said to Trevor. "Devon wanted to be just like you." Kayla glanced back at the fire. "And then you started all this shit."

Trevor turned his back on us. He watched the flames but did nothing to put them out.

Fire Chief Wallis and his team arrived in the fire truck and quickly set up the hoses. Within minutes they had the fire under control.

I held up my camera to get Jim's attention and, as his crew worked, the chief approached me. "Who is it?" he asked. "Who set this fire?" He glanced at Kayla, but I shook my head. I showed him the photos on my camera, of Trevor starting the fire. I didn't have to say a word.

Anger reddened the chief's face as he stared Trevor down. When Trevor finally looked away, Jim took him by the arm and pulled him aside. Trevor didn't try to run or defend himself as the chief gave him hell. For a moment he almost appeared relieved that he had been caught. Perhaps he was.

Kayla, on the other hand, looked just as heartbroken as the chief. "I don't think Devon will ever forgive me," she told me. "Trevor will go to jail. It's my fault."

"There's nothing to forgive," I said. "You did the right thing. Someone had to stop Trevor. Devon will understand. The chief will help him understand."

Trevor was now in tears. Suddenly, I felt bad for him. His first impulse had been to do the right thing. He had wanted to build his firefighting skills. But now he had lost everything—the respect of his team and his community.

I walked over and put my hand on his muscled upper arm to comfort him. "You will get through this," I assured him.

He shook me off. "We're done," he said.

I realized at that point he was angry. He was angry at me, his brother and Kayla. The thing is, he wasn't angry at himself. Matt was right. Devon was more mature than his big brother. Trevor acted like a lost teen, not a grown man.

I stepped back and looked him over. He didn't seem so attractive anymore. "You're right," I said finally. "We are done."

TWELVE

First thing the next morning, I stopped in at Tommy's Café. My excuse was to pick up coffee, but I was really there to see Fire Chief Wallis and, more important, Matt. They were sitting together at the counter, as I knew they would be.

"Claire," said Matt, nodding at me. He didn't look too pleased with me.

"Matt," I said.

"I guess congratulations are in order," the chief said. "You caught the real firebug."

"I certainly don't feel like celebrating," I said.

Jim grunted. "Me neither."

"So what happens to Trevor now?" I asked the chief. "Jail time, I expect."

"We've suspended him from service at the fire department, obviously," Jim told me. "He's been charged on seven counts of arson. I suspect he was responsible for many more fires than we know about. Remember all those garbage can and dumpster fires over the last three years?"

"I thought those were started by some dumb kid," Matt said.

"We all did," said Jim.

"I still don't get why Trevor did it," I said. "I dated the guy for nearly a month, but it's like I didn't know anything about him. If I hadn't seen it for myself, I never would have believed he started those fires."

"Don't beat yourself up," said Jim. "Trevor had us all fooled."

"Did Trevor have a history of setting fires?" I asked the chief. "Did he burn things as a kid?"

Jim shook his head. "Not as far as we can tell. He told the cops he started setting the fires only after he became a firefighter. His brother said the same thing."

"He said at first he set those fires because he wanted to train himself," I told Jim. "He wanted to be a better firefighter."

"The funny thing is, I believe him," said Jim. "I never saw a more dedicated firefighter. He loved his job. He wanted to be the best." He paused. "He *was* the best. He could have gone pro, got a job as a professional firefighter in the city."

"So why did he do it?" I asked. "Why did he set those fires? Even after he tried to explain it to me, I still can't make sense of it."

"I can tell you why," said Matt.

The chief and I both turned to look at him.

"When I get a call that someone is missing, I feel a thrill," Matt told us. "I'm worried, of course. I hate to see anyone lost, but I still feel that rush of excitement. Very often the missing person is found right away, and there is no search. I actually feel disappointment then. I go home and don't know what to do with myself."

The chief nodded in agreement. "As firefighters, we spend most of our volunteer time fixing equipment or washing the truck," he said. "The men are *wishing* for a fire so they can do something."

"So Trevor set the fires to release that tension," I said.

The chief sighed. "I'm going to sit down with my fire crew and have a long talk. We'll have to come up with ways for them to deal with those feelings. I won't let this happen again."

"Trevor also liked being the hero," I said.

"We all do," said Matt.

I tucked my arm through his. "Listen, Matt, I'm really sorry about the way I acted this past week. I guess I got a kick out of you and Trevor fighting over me. I liked the attention."

"I understand."

"The thing is, I never really liked Trevor," I said. "I just liked the *idea* of Trevor, that a firefighter wanted me." I paused. "I've always been interested in you."

"I know," he said.

"You knew?"

"I could tell from that smoldering look you give me."

I snuggled closer to him and gave him another one of those smoldering looks. "Are you saying I was on fire for you?"

Matt grinned back at me. "Hey, where there's smoke, there's fire."

By the age of eighteen, **GAIL ANDERSON-DARGATZ** knew she wanted to write about women in rural settings. Today, Gail is a bestselling author. *A Recipe for Bees* and *The Cure for Death by Lightning* were finalists for the Scotiabank Giller Prize. She also teaches other authors how to write fiction. Gail lives in the Shuswap region of British Columbia, the landscape found in so much of her writing.

Playing with Fire is the follow-up to *Search and Rescue*. Her next Claire Abbott mystery will be published in 2016. For more information, visit www.gailanderson-dargatz.ca.

When a young woman goes missing on a nature trail, small-town journalist Claire Abbott is first on the scene, as usual. The clues to the woman's whereabouts are misleading, but Claire has a sixth sense—what the fire chief calls a "radar for crime." She's more than just a journalist chasing a story. Claire is determined to do the right thing at any cost.

Search and Rescue is the first novel in a series of mysteries featuring journalist and sleuth Claire Abbott.

"[A] relatable character, and [Claire's] psychic ability grows at just the right pace for a short series opener." —*Booklist*

RAPID READS
WWW.RAPID-READS.COM

Nicole Charles didn't go to journalism school to become a gossip columnist. More than anything, she wants to be a real reporter, but it looks like she's never going to get a chance.

Then one night while covering a gallery opening, she discovers a dead body in a dark alley. An up-and-coming artist has been stabbed in the throat with an antique icepick. Nicole is right in the middle of the biggest story of the year. It's the chance of a lifetime. Too bad someone had to die to make it happen.

"Richards hooks the reader within thirty seconds: west coast Vancouver atmosphere, tight plot, judicious back story, dialogue and a body."
—*Don Graves, Canadian Mystery Reviews*

RAPID READS
WWW.RAPID-READS.COM